HODDER CHILDREN'S BOOKS

First published in Great Britain in 2016 by Hodder and Stoughton
This paperback edition published in 2017

A CIP catalogue record for this book
is available from the British Library.

ISBN: 978 1 444 92356 8

10 9 8 7 6 5 4 3 2 1

Printed and bound in China

MIX
Paper from
responsible sources
FSC
www.fsc.org   FSC® C104740

Hodder Children's Books
An imprint of Hachette Children's Group
Part of Hodder and Stoughton
Carmelite House, 50 Victoria Embankment. London EC4Y 0l

An Hachette UK Company
www.hachette.co.uk

www.hachettechildrens.co.uk

LOVE
Matters Most

Mij Kelly & Gerry Turley

Hodder
Children's
Books

Why is the bear staring into the night,
at a world that is turning shimmering white?

The wind's full of snow. The air's full of frost.

She's looking for something, but what has she lost?

And why would a bear go out in a storm,
leaving a cave that's sheltered and warm?

It must be important. Is she searching for gold...

or ruby-red berries out there in the cold...

or the forest's true magic dancing in light?
Why is she out on such a cold night?

Will she catch silver salmon leaping the weir...

or watch as a snowflake melts to a tear...

or wonder and stop, transfixed in a dream
by faraway stars that glitter and gleam?

No, none of these. There are prints in the snow.
Who could have made them, and where do they go?

She's searching
for someone.
Who could it be?

Look – there's the answer.

Of course, can you see?

Yes, the world's full of treasures and fabulous sights,
   but when bear finds her cub, who was lost in the night,

she cuddles him warm and cuddles him close,
and knows, above all...

that love matters most.